BOOK 3

BILLY IS NASTY TO ANT

D1350145

James Minter

Helen Rushworth - Illustrator

www.thebillybooks.co.uk

MINTER PUBLISHING LIMITED

Minter Publishing Limited (MPL)
4 Lauradale, Bracknell RG12 7DT

Copyright © James Minter 2015

James Minter has asserted his rights under the
Copyright Design, and Patents Act, 1988 to be the author
of this work

PB ISBN: 978-1-910727-126
HB ISBN: 978-1-910727-140

Printed and bound in Great Britain by Ingram Spark,
Milton Keynes

Illustrations copyright © Helen Rushworth

This book is sold subject to the condition that it shall not,
by way of trade or otherwise, be lent, resold, hired out,
or otherwise circulated in any form of binding or cover
other than that in which it is published and without a
similar condition, including this condition, being
imposed on the subsequent purchaser.

>>>>>

*To those whose lives are controlled by
jealousy. Free yourselves.*

>>>>>

This book belongs to

....

I give it

stars

1

END-OF-TERM PROJECT

'Right, class, let's have some quiet.' Miss Tompkins, year five's form teacher, clapped her hands to get their attention.

Best mates Billy, Ant, and Tom shared the same table. As usual, Ant sat telling a joke. He spoke in a soft voice so that Miss wouldn't hear him.

'If it takes one man one week to walk a fortnight, how many apples in a bunch of grapes?' Ant sat back, flashing a big gummy smile. 'Well?'

Billy and Tom exchanged glances, before screwing up their faces in a *what's he talking about?* sort of way.

'You don't know, do you?' Ant grinned from ear to ear. 'It's obvious, two elephants, of course.' He sniggered.

Confused, Billy let out a mocking laugh. 'You're weird.' He spoke at the same time as Miss Tompkins.

'Billy Field, that means you!' Her eyes narrowed, and she raised her voice to make herself heard.

'Sorry, Miss Tompkins.' Billy's face turned red. The colour travelled to the tip of his ears. He did *not* like getting picked out by her; he always liked to think that he was her favourite. The last thing he wanted to do was cause her to get upset.

Billy looked down at his books. 'It's your fault, Ant,' he spoke in a whisper. 'For telling such a stupid joke. Now, you've made Miss shout at me.' Billy eyeballed him.

Miss continued to speak, 'Today, we will start our end-of-term project.' She spoke in a slow, loud voice. 'You will work in groups of three.'

She moved to the front of her desk and leant against a corner. 'You can choose who you want to work with and sit with them.

The sound of chair legs scraping on the wooden floor followed. 'Not yet! Wait until I tell you.' She eyed the class. 'Now, quickly and quietly, move into your groups.'

The noise in the room exploded with the

sound of twenty-seven class members all standing at once. Billy, Ant, and Tom remained seated. As mates, they had always done things together.

'I wonder what we'll get to do.' Tom looked about him and pointed. 'Have you seen Khalid? He's got to work with Julie and Suzanna. Poor him.'

Billy turned to look. 'I hope he likes boy bands. That's all they ever talk about.' He smirked at the thought of Khalid's challenge.

'Okay now,' Miss Tompkins called out to bring calm back to the classroom. 'So, who's working together?'

She walked in the spaces between the tables, taking note of the different groups. 'Please, listen carefully. This project will count toward your individual assessment, but I'm also looking to see which team works best together, and which individual student contributes most to their team's efforts.'

'She still hasn't told us what we're doing.' Billy spoke out of the corner of his mouth so that Miss would not hear, but she did.

'Billy, not again! Now is not the time for talking.' Miss Tompkins held his gaze.

'Sorry, Miss.' He looked away, swallowed up by his embarrassment.

'I need one team member from each group to come to the front.' Miss waved her hand in a 'come here' gesture. 'So, choose who you want to send.'

A flurry of activity followed, as a race of

children headed to her desk. Before Billy and Tom had time to discuss it, Ant had gone. He reached her first.

'Who said it should be him?' Billy asked, wide-eyed and glaring at Tom.

Tom shrugged. 'I dunno; not me.'

Ant returned, waving several sheets of paper. He set them down on the table, and all three boys leant in.

'This is awesome.' Tom continued to read, and his eyes looked like flying saucers. 'Create a TV-style advert. And look, it's a class competition where we get to vote on everyone else's.' He jumped up and down in his seat.

'Yeah, but that means they'll get to vote on ours as well.' Billy pointed to the paper. 'Look, there's an award for the team that produces the most creative thirty-second advert. And for the individual who makes the biggest contribution.' *That will be me*, Billy thought.

'Cor, does it say what we have to advertise?' Tom could hardly get his words out with the excitement.

Before anyone had time to answer, Ant jumped up. 'I know, let's do Rice Krispies. I'll be Snap.' He did a little dance and made snapping sounds. 'You can be Crackle,' he said, pointing at Tom. 'He's got blond hair like yours. And Billy, you can be Pop.'

Miss Tompkins turned around to see what the commotion was, but Ant saw her before she saw him and sat down quickly.

'Phew, that was close.' Ant took a peek to see if she still looked their way. 'So, what do you think?'

'Really? Me as Pop?' Billy arched his eyebrows. 'Why do you say that?'

Ant had no time to answer, as the racket in the classroom climbed to a new level.

Miss Tompkins' voice boomed out, 'I know you're excited, but do you have any questions?' She rubbed the side of her head as if she had a headache.

The teacher peered over the top of her glasses.

'Look.' Billy nodded to Ant and Tom. 'She always does that when there's too much noise.'

Gradually, the other children noticed, and the room fell silent.

Ant sat with his hand thrust high in the air. 'Miss, Miss, Miss.' He felt so determined to get her attention that his bottom hovered above the seat.

'Yes, Anthony? What have you got to say?' The grumpiness in her voice had gone.

'Miss, are we allowed to do the Rice Krispies advert? Please, Miss.'

'I haven't agreed on anything with anyone yet.' She smiled at him. 'Think about it a bit longer. Work out who will do what, and what costumes and equipment you'll need, then decide.'

'Yeah, but I want to be Snap.' Ant jumped up from his chair and danced about.

'That's as may be, Anthony, but you heard what I said.' She rubbed her forehead. 'Please!' The word came out louder than expected, and everyone stared at the teacher.

Ant retook his seat.

'Have you noticed how Ant's been behaving with Miss?' Billy looked at Tom, keeping his back toward Ant so that he wouldn't overhear.

'What do you mean?' Tom looked past Billy and to Ant, who sat busy reading the handout.

Billy slumped back in his chair. 'You know, he keeps going up to her desk, asking her questions and stuff like that. Even though he's made loads of noise, she's been nice to him, but she told me off twice.'

'Maybe she feels sorry for him after he had his bike stolen.' Tom sounded quite matter of fact.

Billy shifted in his seat. He didn't want any reminders of his part in the bike stealing, or for Tom to recall it either. His face reddened again until his cheeks burned.

Billy struggled to speak, 'Yeah, you're probably right.' *But I thought I was her favourite,* Billy kept that bit to himself. 'What about doing an advert for toys, or …' He paused and thought, as he wanted to change the subject. 'I know, what about doing one for games controllers? I wanted a new one for my birthday.'

'Now, class, you've had plenty of time to come up with ideas. Can one member of each group come to my desk—'

The crashing sound of a tumbling chair caused her to stop talking. Ant stood hopping about. In his haste, he had caught his foot on a chair leg and sent it flying. 'Yeeouch.'

Miss Tompkins shook her head in disbelief. 'As I was trying to say, Anthony, can one member from every group come up to my desk and tell me what advert they're planning.'

By the time she had finished speaking, Ant was stood next to her. 'Me, Miss. We … want …' He puffed. '… to … do … the … Rice … Krispies … advert.' He panted so much that he could hardly get his words out.

Miss Tompkins picked up her pen. 'I'd never have guessed.' Beside Billy, Ant, and

Tom's names, she wrote, 'Rice Krispies'.

Ant dashed back to his table, avoiding any furniture or wayward chair legs.

'See, I said she would let us.' He sounded triumphant. Then, seated, he beamed the broadest smile imaginable.

Billy and Tom exchanged glances; they both looked confused. 'So, not toys or game controllers, then?' Billy picked up his pencil and doodled. 'How come you decided? Who made you the leader?'

Tom wanted to keep the peace. 'Yeah, but he did have the idea first, and he's done all the running up and down to Miss.'

'Come on.' Ant wouldn't be put off. He got out a pen and blank sheet of paper and drew a shape like a stage. 'So, what do we need?' He looked at his two mates in turn.

'A box of Rice Krispies,' Tom said.

'And a bowl,' Billy said, helpfully.

'And milk. I like lots of milk on mine.' Ant wrote a list. 'What about costumes? Snap, Crackle, and Pop each wear a different colour.'

As Ant spoke, Billy shut his eyes, trying to remember what colours Snap, Crackle, and Pop wore. He couldn't. 'I think we'd better watch some TV tonight to remind ourselves.'

'Their costumes won't be easy to make.' Tom groaned.

All three nodded.

2

GRANDAD, HIS NAME IS POP

Billy arrived at his grandad's. He always went there after school to wait for his mum or dad to come home from work. His dog Jacko stayed with grandad during the day also. When Billy came in the back door, the dog jumped up to greet him, and his tail wagged furiously.

'So, Billy, how did school go today?' His grandad asked the same question every day. Usually, Billy answered in the same way: *Okay, I suppose*, but not today.

'Grandad, I've got to watch telly. Miss says so.' Billy ran straight from the back door to the front room without stopping, leaving a trail of discarded school stuff in his wake. Jacko raced after him.

'Billy,' his grandad called. 'What do you mean, "Miss says so"?'

'It's for our end-of-term project. We're doing a Rice Krispies advert, and I need to watch it to remind myself how it goes.' Billy's voice faded while he moved further away from the kitchen and toward the living room.

'Whose idea was that?' Grandad fumbled with his hearing aid as he set off to catch up with Billy.

'Ant said it first,' Billy called back. 'And he decided who should be which one, but I can't remember what they look like.'

'Remember what who looks like?' Grandad reached the front room. His brow creased as he tried to work out what Billy was talking about.

'You know, the Rice Krispy kids—Snap, Crackle, and Pop.'

Grandad put his hand to his ear; his hearing aid still played up. 'Snack, Cackle, and Plop? They're strange names.'

'*Snap*, *Crackle,* and *Pop*, Grandad. You know nothing for someone as old as you.' Billy giggled.

'I'll give you old,' Grandad teased, ruffling Billy's hair. 'That's the BBC you're watching.' He pointed at the television. 'You'll find no adverts on there.'

'I know, but I like *Blue Peter*.'

'Well, it won't help with Snack, Cackle, and Plop. Have you looked at the cereals in the kitchen? I might even have a box. You'll need a chair; they're in the cupboard above the microwave.'

Billy's eyes didn't leave the screen. Jacko came and sat on the ground beside him, leaning against his legs.

'It's educational. They tell you loads of good things. And Jacko likes watching their dog.' Billy laughed.

'I know; I used to watch it with your mum. They had Petra then.'

'What? When she was a kid? That's years ago!'

'Don't sound so surprised; even I was a child once.' Grandad closed his eyes as he tried to remember what being a child felt like.

Billy noticed and switched channels, looking for adverts.

'Mum, it's not fair.' Max, Ant's younger sister, ran from room to room to find her mother. 'Ant says Miss told him to watch TV. I bet she didn't.'

She got no reply, and couldn't find her mother. 'Mum, Muuuuum?' Max ran upstairs, 'Where are you?'

'What's happened?' Her mum appeared on the landing, carrying a laundry basket. 'Why all the shouting?'

'It's Ant. He says Miss told him to watch telly. I bet he's making it up.'

'Surprisingly, he's not. Well, I don't think so, at least.' Max's mum walked on toward the airing cupboard. 'He told me he has to make an advert for a project, and so he needs to watch TV. He'll soon be finished.'

She spoke to no one, as Max had run back downstairs to quiz Ant about what he had to do.

Max joined Ant, seated on the sofa. The TV showed an advert for Cornflakes.

'Cock-a-doodle-do,' Max said while she looked at him.

Ant stared back but said nothing.

'That's the noise cockerels make, like the one on the Cornflakes box.' Max beamed. 'You'll have to do that when you make your advert.'

'Maybe if we were making a cornflakes

ad, but we're not.' Ant slid off the sofa and onto the floor. Then, grabbing his toy box, he emptied it. Building bricks, marbles, plastic figures, and model cars lay scattered about the place.

'You wait 'til Mum sees this mess. She won't be happy.' Max picked up a plastic figure dressed in a red top with a cobweb drawn on it, a red hood with grey patches for eyes, tight blue leggings, and red boots. She held it up to the light for a better look before putting it back.

'What have you lost?' Max asked, now more curious than ever.

'Snap, Crackle, and Pop. I'm sure I've got some plastic figures. Me, Billy, and Tom have to do a Rice Krispies advert. We need to dress up and act it out.'

He sorted through the pile of toys. 'Ah, I knew I had one.' He held up Pop, dressed in his yellow hat, red jacket, and cut-off blue trousers.

Max got on the floor beside him and sorted through the muddle.

'Here.' She held up Snap. 'He wears a chef's hat, red scarf, yellow jacket, and jeans.' She pointed to each item in turn. 'Where will you get a chef's hat from?'

'Mum will know,' Ant said. After a further rummage, he found Crackle. 'I knew I had all three.' He lined them up on the low table positioned beside the sofa.

'Now, you don't need to watch telly, do you?' Max waved the TV remote control around.

'Hey, not so fast; I still need to see the

advert.'

'No, you don't. You're just saying that. Look at the figures; you can see what they're wearing.'

'Yeah, but I can't remember the words.'

Ant snatched at the controller, but Max tossed it onto the sofa. He made a grab for it, pushing her aside.

'Ow, that hurt.' Max rubbed her arm.

'Children, what are you doing? Ant, mind your sister.' Their mum stood in the doorway.

'He started it.' Max glowered at Ant.

'That may well be, but I'm finishing it. Come on, you two; it's time for tea.'

'Oh, great. What are we having, Mum?' Before he had finished speaking, Ant had sat up at the kitchen table.

Max joined him.

'I thought you'd like a bowl of cereal; Rice Krispies, maybe.' Ant's mum had a mischievous grin on her face.

'Really?' Ant liked the idea of having breakfast for tea; a sort of upside-down day.

'No, not really. You've got spaghetti hoops on toast.'

'In ancient times, Rice Krispies were best friends with the dinosaurs ...' The sound of the telly drifted into the kitchen.

'Quick, Ant, it's on!' Max ran back toward the living room.

'Hit record,' Ant shouted after her. He arrived in the room moments later. 'Did you get it?'

'I think so.' She stopped recording and pressed play. 'Fingers crossed.'

Both children sat on the floor to watch. When the advert ended, Ant dropped his head into his hands.

'Dinosaurs? How will we ever get a dinosaur? That'll be way too difficult.'

3

BUT THEY ... WHAT?

Billy stood beside his mum, who, as Deputy Head Teacher of the secondary school, sat busy marking a pile of essays. 'Mum, can you sew?'

'Yes, but not right now. Can't you see I've got this lot to finish?' She waved her hand over the stack of school books. 'Why? What do you need?'

'Stuff for our end-of-term project. We're doing an advert for Rice Krispies, and I need a Pop costume.' Billy glanced over her shoulder. 'Wow, will I have to do that when I get to secondary school?'

'This is year-nine work. You'll get homework every night. Now, this Pop costume, what exactly do you need?'

'I saw the ad on Grandad's TV. Pop wears a yellow peaked hat, a red jacket like a soldier at Buckingham Palace with that gold string stuff over the shoulders …'

'Epaulettes, I think you mean. You'll need to ask Grandad about them; he was in the army.'

'… A black belt, blue cut-off trousers, black boots, and pixie ears. … Oh, and he has his name in big red letters on his hat.' Billy rolled his eyes upward while he tried to remember if that covered it all.

'How long have I got to get this costume sorted?' His mum looked at her pile of marking and hoped it wouldn't become an overnight project.

'A couple of weeks, I think, but I'd like it quicker,' Billy said.

'Yes, Sir. Right, Sir. We'll see what we can do.' His mum made a salute. 'I'll jump to it right away.'

'Muuummm, stop messing. I meant, well, can you get it done sooner?'

'You can start by going to your bedroom and seeing what bits of the costume you can find there. And take this hairy thing with you.' His mum looked down at Jacko, who had settled under her desk. The dog snuffed and snorted before lifting himself onto his front legs and stretching.

'Come on, Jacko; we know when we're not wanted.' Billy turned back to face his mum. 'It needs to look fantastic. I want to win the end-of-term prize, to make you, dad, and grandad proud.'

'Yeah, well, I'm sure we can do something, apart from the pixie ears.'

Ant sat in front of the television with a pad of paper on his knee, a pencil in one hand, and the remote control in the other. He pressed the play button.

'... *but they were* ...' He hit stop and picked up his pencil to write.

'But they ... what?' He pressed rewind before pressing play again.

'*... but they were ...*'

He grabbed his pencil and wrote 'were'. The advert continued to play.

'... *they asked the T-Rex if he could put a roar inside them ...*'

'I've missed loads now. What was after were?' He rewound again. 'This is hopeless.' He yelled for Max, 'Sis?'

Max came and stood beside him. 'What, Bro?'

'I need your help.'

She looked at him.

'Please.' Ant grunted and shot her a cheesy grin. 'I need to get the words to the advert, but I can't write and work the recorder at the same time.'

Max took the controller. 'It didn't record from the beginning, did it? You still need to see the start.' She pressed play.

'... *but they were so small ...*'

'Stop! I wasn't ready.' Ant threw down his pen. 'Wait 'til I say go.'

'I'm only trying to help.' Max rewound the recording yet again. 'Are you ready now?' She looked at him for a response.

'I've got "but they were". Can you play the recording to there and stop.'

She pressed play, but the advert continued beyond 'were'.

'Stop! Didn't you hear "but they were"?' He glared at his sister.

'Yeah, but my finger slipped off the button.'

'This will take forever. I wish I hadn't suggested Rice Krispies now.' He crashed his notepad onto the low table, sending Snap, Crackle, and Pop on an unexpected journey across the room.

'… So small that the dinosaurs …' Max repeated the words of the advert.

'What are you going on about?'

'The next lot of words—I remember them.'

Ant picked up the pad and pen and wrote them down. 'Are you sure?'

'Listen.' Max pressed play, and they both listened. 'See, I knew I had it right.'

'Sorry, Sis.'

'And the next ones say, "would sometimes stand on them".' Max looked at Ant. 'What are you waiting for?'

Ant busied himself with writing, and soon they had completed the whole script except for the beginning.

'Thanks, Max, but can you help with the

start of the ad as well?' He shoved over for her before turning back to live TV.

They waited, watched, and listened until the advert came on again. Soon, they had all the words.

'Now, I need to write them nice and neat so that Billy and Tom can read them.' Quietly, Ant recited them to himself. 'I still don't feel sure what to do about a T-Rex.' Deep in thought, a glazed look came over his face.

'Oh, that's easy,' Max said. 'You're doing this with Billy, so why not use Jacko? Remember the advert? That dinosaur rex had those spiky things on its back. You could make some from painted paper.' Max skipped around the room. 'See, all you had to do was ask me.'

'That's a great idea, but it needs to be cardboard. Paper will flop over. Come on; let's watch the recording again so that I can see what else we need.'

4

JACKOSAURUS REX

Billy stood in front of his bedroom mirror. He turned first one way, then the other, trying to get a good look at himself in his Pop costume.

'Mum?' he called out, hoping she stood nearby. 'Mum, I can't see my back. Is my hat all right and those "eplet" things? They look more like a pile of string. How will I win a prize looking like an undone knot?' He turned back the other way, screwing his neck so far around that his hat fell off. 'Mum?'

'Billy, stop shouting. I've got to get ready for school as well, and what about Jacko? If you want to take him with you, you'll need to walk to school.' She wandered along the corridor toward his bedroom while she spoke.

'Did you hear me?' Billy's mum put her head around his door and burst out laughing. 'What's happened to you?'

'It's not funny. I know Ant's mum's been so busy with his costume, and Tom's, too.'

'Yes, well, I've had a stack of marking to do, and end-of-term reports.' Billy's mum reached out to straighten his epaulettes and fix his hat on again. 'You'll be all right. Anyway, everyone will look at Jacko. Just make sure you read your lines nice and clearly.'

'Read? I've learnt them off by heart. We've only got two lines each, and even I can remember them. I just need to keep Jacko from running off.'

At the mention of his name, Jacko appeared at Billy's bedroom entrance. The dog barged in and pushed the door open wide; his dinosaur spines looked incredibly wonky. He had chewed the string that Billy had used to hold them in place. It no longer ran from his collar to a loop around his tail, but instead, dragged behind him.

Unlike Billy, he didn't care about end-of-term prizes. 'Jacko, what have you done?'

Billy looked up at his mum. 'I'll never win.' He slumped facedown onto his bed, knocking his hat off again.

'Well, you won't, behaving like that.

Come on; get your costume off, and Jacko's.' His mum lifted him into a sitting position. 'You'll need to carry them both to school.'

Ant arrived at school first, and got in line outside the classroom. The boy carried several plastic bags, containing his costume and the props needed for the project. Excited, he waited for Miss Tompkins to unlock the door.

'You're nice and early, Anthony. Do you feel ready for your performance?' Miss Tompkins held open the door for him. 'The other teachers thought it might be fun to get two groups to act out their adverts on the assembly hall stage. That way, the whole school can enjoy them.' She smiled down at him. 'Is that okay? What do you think?'

'Yesss … I suppose so.' The tremble in his voice suggested that he didn't feel so sure.

'Are you certain? You don't sound so sure.'

He thought for a second. 'Do you mean the whole school, in front of everyone? Wow! Great.' A charge of excitement shot down his spine.

'From what I've seen, I know you'll be fine, and you've got Tom and Billy.'

'And Jacko.' Ant said, nodding and grinning.

'Jacko?' Lines appeared on Miss' forehead.

'Yeah, Billy's golden retriever. He's the

dinosaur rex.' Ant said it as if it were an everyday thing.

'A dog as a dinosaur? I hope he's well behaved.' Miss Tompkins raised her eyebrows with a look of disbelief. 'Is he housetrained?'

'Ask him yourself.' Ant pointed to the classroom door.

Jacko had shoved open the door, yanking Billy in behind him.

'Hi, Jacko.' Ant clapped. 'Come on, then.'

The eager dog didn't need a second invitation. He bounded across the room, tugging the lead out of Billy's hand.

Ant bent. 'You're going to be a famous actor.' He ruffled the dog's fur. 'The whole school will be watching.'

The dog ran in a circle, chasing his tail, and as he did, he wrapped the lead around Miss Tompkins' ankles.

'Don't move, Miss.' Ant knelt to free her.

'Billy, can't you keep your dog under control?' Miss sounded unhappy.

'Sorry, Miss. It's all new to him, and he's excited.' Billy grabbed at Jacko's collar and held him tight.

By now, the classroom had filled with children.

Miss Tomkins gestured to everyone for quiet. 'The teachers have decided that two groups should perform their adverts right after morning assembly. Anthony has volunteered his group. Who else wants to do it?'

Julie looked at her classmates before

putting her hand up. 'We'll do it, Miss.'

'Great, thank you, Julie. Can you and Anthony's group take your things to the hall? The rest of the class will come along in a few minutes.'

Backstage, Julie, Suzanna, and Khalid huddled around their bags, pulling off their school uniforms in favour of costumes, reciting lines and sorting props. Ant, Billy, Tom, and Jacko stood off to one side, doing much the same. Both groups, apart from Ant, looked a bit fearful at their impending stage debut.

It didn't help when Miss Tompkins informed them, 'There are more than five-hundred children and teachers out there, and some parents.'

'Epic.' Ant turned to high-five Billy and Tom. Neither returned the gesture. 'Come on; this is fun.' He bounced from foot to foot. 'Jacko's keen.' He looked down at the dog, who had settled for a sleep. 'He just doesn't like to show it.' Ant's eyes grew wide. 'That reminds me. What do you call a sleeping dinosaur?'

'We haven't got time for one of your senseless jokes.' Billy struggled with his epaulettes. 'Stupid things.'

'A dino-snore!' Ant let out a deafening snort.

Tom tutted. 'Not funny.'

'Yeah, but the good news is that Julie, Khalid, and Suzanna will go first. Miss just told me. Oh, and Billy, make sure that Jacko doesn't eat all the Rice Krispies.' Ant wandered off.

'He's enjoying this.' Tom smiled as he watched his friend walk away.

Before Billy could react, the voice of the school's head teacher, Mrs Johnston, blasted through the speakers. She addressed the assembly from the stage on the other side of the closed stage curtains. Everyone stopped to listen.

'As an end-of-term treat, some of Miss Tompkins' year five class will perform for us this morning. Their project work is to recreate a television advert here on stage.' She beckoned to year five's teacher. 'Miss Tompkins will introduce each team in turn.'

Miss Tompkins joined the head teacher, standing in front of the curtains.

'Thank you, Mrs Johnston. First up, we have Julie, Khalid, and Suzanna doing a Haribo advert. So, please stay quiet, and be prepared to be entertained.'

Both women set off toward the side of the stage. They clapped as they walked, while the heavy, deep red velvet stage curtains opened behind them.

On stage, Khalid and Julie sat at a table, looking out into the audience. They had dressed like mums and dads as office workers in a meeting. Khalid wore a white shirt with a blue striped tie, glasses, and a false beard. He looked more like a dad than a schoolboy. Julie had donned spectacles— the half-round sort—so that she could look over the top like Miss Tompkins. She also wore her school blouse and skirt.

Suzanna stood off to one side. She had on a white blouse with the collar over the lapel of her dark blue jacket. Also, she'd borrowed a pair of her mother's high-heeled shoes, which made her look extra tall. Clasped in her hand, she had a packet of Haribo sweets. They would do the advert where the adults pretended to be children.

Suzanna walked over to the table and scattered several sweets. She opened the dialogue first, 'I just want to talk about these Haribo Starmix sweets.' Suzanna spoke in a pretend little girl's voice.

Julie picked up a heart-shaped sweet and held it up. 'I like the hearts 'cos they make me feel loved.' She looked at the other two.

Her imitation toddler voice made them smile, and the audience laughed out loud.

Khalid picked up a sweet. 'And, also, I liked the rings.' His voice came out all high and squeaky.

'And the gold bears,' Suzanna said.

'Because it looks like a ring, when they go swimming, so they don't drown,' Khalid said in his shrill child's voice with added extreme swimmer's arm movements. Everyone roared with laughter; so much so that no one heard Suzanna's last line.

On cue, the curtains closed, and the sound of all three children singing the Haribo song came through the speakers. The hall went quiet; the audience focused on the stage. Khalid, Julie, and Suzanna walked through the curtains and took a bow; everyone clapped loudly. Miss Tompkins left her chair and reached the children on centre stage.

'Well, we weren't expecting that,' their teacher declared. 'Well done!' Then, with another smile, she asked, 'Did you see this advert on television?' The teacher looked around to see if anyone could confirm. 'Or did you make it up?'

'Please, Miss, it's on telly and the internet. We, well, Khalid found it, when we went searching for ads,' Julie told her.

Suzanna and Khalid nodded their agreement.

'I think you'll all agree that it was a great start to year five's advert project. Now, let's see what Anthony, Tom, and Billy can do.' Miss gestured for the others to leave.

'Come on, Billy; we're on in a minute.' Ant checked his costume before pouring out a bowl of Rice Krispies. He placed it on a long table in the centre of the stage, behind the closed curtains. 'You'll need to get Jacko to stand at the far end.'

Ant looked at the dog, who now sat very alert after the Haribo advert. 'Jacko, remember to stand on the Krispies but don't eat them.' He addressed his words to the dog but meant them for Billy.

'All right, I know.' Billy yanked at the strap that held his hat in place. It had slipped to one side again. 'Jacko, stop pulling.' The smell of the Krispies had attracted the dog's attention. Billy looked pale and nervous; he held the dog tight.

'Tom, you stand at the other end of the table from Jacko,' Ant commanded. 'And hold the box of Rice Krispies so that it faces the front. That way, everyone can see it.' He looked at Tom for a response.

'Okay.' Tom sprayed Rice Krispies when he spoke.

Ant shook his head, 'My mum always says don't talk with your mouth full.'

'I just need to swallow.' Tom pushed his hand into the box for another scoop.

'Don't eat all the cereal.' Ant snatched at the box, 'I need to scatter some on the table for our Jackosaurus Rex to walk on. Remember the words?'

Tom diverted the scoop of Krispies heading for his mouth to Ant's outstretched hand.

'That's better,' Ant said. 'Right, Billy. Take Jacko and stand him on the table. Tom, get to the other end. I'll stay here in the middle.' Ant spoke quietly, 'Listen, Miss is introducing us now.' He picked up the microphone, as he would be the first to speak.

From the other side of the closed curtain, they could hear Miss Tompkins. Billy loped over to the curtains, which separated them from the audience. With his fingers, he eased back the material and peeked out. Through the small gap, the boys could see Max seated a few rows back.

Miss Tompkins drew near to the end of her introduction. 'Anthony, Tom, and Billy's advert is called, "How they got sound into Rice Krispies" ... Curtains, please.' The teacher headed off stage.

Slowly, the heavy material moved to each side. The boys looked out over a sea of faces, which stared back at them. A wave of nerves went through Ant, in a good way. His stomach tightened, and he swallowed hard. *Come on; you can do this*, he thought.

He brought the microphone up close to his mouth; so close that he hit it against his top lip. The thud echoed around the hall, and a series of sniggers came from the audience. *Don't mess up now*, he told himself.

Ant looked over at Miss Tompkins, who smiled and tilted her head as a sign that it was okay to begin.

He spoke slowly, loudly, and clearly: 'In ancient times, Rice Krispies were best friends with the dinosaurs.' The large hall echoed with his words.

Billy held Jacko tight so that he couldn't eat any of the Krispies. The dog's dark green spines looked striking against his golden fur.

Ant passed Billy the microphone; he was next to speak. As Billy reached out to take it, one of his epaulettes flopped forward. Without thinking, he grabbed at it and let go of the dog's lead.

No longer feeling a pull on his collar, Jacko took flight. He had heard Max in the audience talking to her fifth-best-friend Katie. With two bounds, the dog had jumped off the table, and then off the stage. He made straight for Max, sitting three rows back.

Like an army commando, Jacko flattened himself to the ground. Then, using his front paws, he dragged himself under rows of squealing children and arrived at Max's feet. The dinosaur spines got ripped off his back and lay in tatters behind him. He gazed up at her with his large, brown puppy-dog eyes and lolling tongue. The dog looked as though he lay there smiling.

'Hi, Jacko.' Max couldn't resist a stroke, but she added quickly, 'You shouldn't be here. Go on, shoo. You're the dinosaur rex.' She looked for the spines, 'Well, not anymore!'

🐾 🐾

'Jacko, here, now,' Billy called out at the top of his voice. Then he leapt off the stage and hit the floor with a thump. His Pop hat fell to the ground, and both epaulettes fell forward at the same time. He looked as though a plate of spaghetti had been poured over him. 'Jacko!'

He ran to the end of the row of chairs where Max sat. 'Grab his collar,' he shouted, talking to no one in particular. Billy shuffled along the row, avoiding overweight school bags stuffed full of books, lunchboxes, and gym kits. He reached Max.

'Come on, you,' he said to Jacko. Billy believed that he ought to feel angry, but in reality, he couldn't. He loved his dog, and no harm had been done. Jacko had only behaved liked his affectionate, playful self.

5

PRIZE WINNERS

Billy arrived back at school minus Jacko and the Pop costume. He had dropped the dog off with his grandad and changed into jeans and a hoody that he had left there for after school. By the time he reached his classroom, the other groups had acted out their adverts. He walked in to a round of applause, not for him, but for the final performance.

'Right, year five,' Miss Tompkins called out. She spotted Billy sneaking in at the back. 'That was the last of the groups, so on your score sheet, mark each performance out of ten ... Billy—' She looked directly at him, '—since you missed all the performances, can you collect up the completed score sheets and bring them to me, please?'

Within a few minutes, the noise in the room rose.

'It sounds like you've all finished.' Miss Tompkins scanned the class. 'Billy, have you collected all the scores?'

'Yes, Miss.' He stood by his desk, busy organising them into a neat pile. 'Coming, Miss.'

'Now, class, I'll need to add up the marks, so please get out your reading books, and no talking.' Impatient, she waved her arm in Billy's direction.

'We won't win,' Ant whispered, sounding despondent. 'Not after Jacko jumped off the stage.' He held his head in his hands. 'We didn't even get a chance to do the whole thing.' He watched Billy out of the corner of his eye, as his friend headed back toward him.

'Come on, Ant. It's not Jacko's fault, or Billy's. Dogs do crazy things; you've seen all those videos on YouTube.' Tom looked up at Billy when he took a seat. 'How's Jacko?' he asked. Tom wore his usual grin. 'Did you make it home or did he try another escape?' He laughed as he spoke.

Billy didn't answer. The three lads sat in silence, pretending to read their books, not knowing what to say to each other.

'Anthony Turner,' Miss Tompkins looked straight at him. 'Come to my desk, please.' For the second time that day, Ant's stomach tightened, and he swallowed hard.

'That doesn't sound good.' He gulped, exchanging glances with Tom and Billy. 'Coming, Miss.'

He slid his chair from beneath the table, careful not to make any noise. Twenty-nine pairs of eyes followed his every move. The walk to Miss Tompkins' desk seemed to take ages.

Ant hesitated, and his mind raced with each step. *What have I done? I mean, apart from the obvious, and that wasn't my fault.* He took another step and another. Finally, he drew closer to his teacher, who sat peering over the top of her glasses. Not a good sign.

'Come on.' She sounded impatient. 'Follow me.' Then, leaving her desk, she headed for the door. Her pace brisk. 'Quickly.'

With the classroom door closed behind them, Miss Tompkins' and Ant's silhouettes were visible through the frosted glass. After a couple of minutes, they returned: Miss Tompkins to her desk, and Ant to his seat. She had decided it best to tell him first that he had won a prize rather than announce it to the class.

'Well?' Tom had to know.

'I can't say.'

'Come on; we're your mates,' Billy joined in.

'Just wait.' Ant's ear-to-ear grin told them it wasn't bad news, whatever she had said.

Miss Tompkins left her chair to perch on the front of her desk. She held out a sheet of paper for everyone to see.

'Here is the list of adverts and the scores you awarded them.' The teacher moved it left and right so that they could all get a look. Unfortunately, the writing proved too small for anyone to see unless they had magnifying vision superpowers.

'Before I announce the winners, I'd like to say to the whole class what a tremendous effort you all made. Over the last two weeks, I've seen you busying yourselves with your ideas and slowly turning them into excellent performances, as we saw today. You all deserve a round of applause.' She clapped, encouraging the class to join in.

'Now, we need to say a special well done to Julie, Khalid, and Suzanna for their extremely comical advert, and because they volunteered to do it in front of the whole school. That takes courage.' She clapped once again. 'Adding up your scores, it seems that you agreed. The Haribo Starmix advert is the clear winner.'

Julie let out a squeak of delight, and Suzanna clasped her hands to her face. Her eyes and mouth went wide open, showing her surprise. Khalid punched the air several times, shouting, 'Yes!' The excitement of winning had taken over.

'If you three would like to come up here to collect your book tokens.' Miss

Tompkins waved gift cards at them.

Billy looked solemn. 'Flipping Jacko. Why did he have to chase after Max?'

'I thought Khalid was hilarious,' Tom said. 'I liked his beard and glasses.'

Miss Tompkins clapped her hands to regain the attention of the class.

'As well as a group prize, I told you I would look to see which student made the most effort toward their team's success. I've made my decision.'

Ant bounced around in his seat. He knew what was coming next.

'Over the last two weeks, the student who has shown the greatest effort is …' Miss Tompkins waited, her pause heightening the excitement. '… Anthony Turner.'

Before the words had left her mouth, Ant had leapt to his feet and did his Snap dance.

He had practiced his moves since Miss Tompkins agreed to let them do the Rice Krispies advert. Disappointed that they had never had the chance to finish their performance, he felt determined to do the dance now.

'Thank you, Anthony.' Miss Tompkins watched with the rest of the children while Ant bounced, wiggled, and snapped his way to her desk. 'Clearly, you're pleased to have won.' She handed him his gift card.

The end-of-lesson bell sounded. 'Right, class, I'll see you after the half-term break.'

6

BILLY IS HORRIBLE TO ANT

By the time that Ant returned to his seat, Billy had vanished without saying anything.

'You seen Billy?' Ant asked Tom.

'Nope. I was speaking to Khalid.'

Ant looked around the classroom but saw no sign of him. 'He's probably gone to his grandad's to collect Jacko.' Ant picked up his costume and props, 'You coming, Tom?'

Billy ran all the way from school to his grandad's. He didn't want to see or talk to anyone. Upon reaching the back door, he stopped and listened. *I hope Grandad's having a sleep*, he thought.

He turned the handle ever so gently to make sure he didn't wake his grandad. With care, he inched open the door and placed his foot through the widening crack. From the other side came a gold-coloured furry snout with a black nose, accompanied by a sniffing and drumming sound. Rhythmically, Jacko's wagging tail beat against the side of the cupboard.

'Shush, Jacko; it's only me.' Billy pushed open the door. 'Where's Grandad?' He didn't expect Jacko to answer, as he had asked the question of himself more than anyone else.

Grandad walked into the kitchen. 'Ah, Billy, I didn't hear you come in. So, how did school go today?' He filled the kettle. 'Do you want a drink?'

'No.'

'No?'

'No, thanks, I mean.'

'Well, did you win?' Grandad knew the answer already from the sullen look on Billy's face. 'Hey, lad, you can't come first all the time. You have to give others a chance.' Grandad placed an arm around Billy's shoulders. 'You'll have other times. You wait and see.'

'After Jacko's antics, I didn't expect to win.'

'So, what's the problem?'

'Ant won a prize.' Billy kicked at the table leg as he spoke.

'What? And you didn't? How come? Weren't you in the same group?'

'Miss gave out two prizes: one for the team who made the best advert, and one for the person who worked the hardest.' Billy kept his eyes cast down. He kicked his feet continually.

'Enough.' Grandad held out his hand to stop Billy's legs from swinging.

'And you say Ant won.' Grandad filled the teapot. 'I bet you'll have a biscuit.' He took down the tin that Billy had known all his life. Tall and round with an airtight top, pictures of different biscuits decorated it, including Billy's favourites—custard creams.

'No, thanks.' Billy slunk off toward the sitting room.

Grandad took his tea and biscuits and joined his grandson on the sofa. Jacko lay at their feet, keeping a close eye on the biscuits in case a crumb fell his way.

'What will you do?' Grandad rubbed Billy's shoulder. He wanted to show him that it was okay to feel upset, and that he was there to support his grandson.

'There's nothing I can do. Ant won the prize, and he's Miss Tompkins' favourite. It's not fair. I brought Jacko to be the dinosaur, and I had a costume and everything. I even learnt my words.' Billy gazed at the television without really watching it.

'In ancient times, Rice Krispies were best friends with the dinosaurs ...' The sound of the advert jolted Billy back into the room. He grabbed the remote control, stabbing at the change channel button.

'I was sure I would win.' His lips tightened. 'Ant didn't do anything that I couldn't have.' Billy folded his arms across his chest, and the remote control fell to the ground. He kicked it hard, sending it across the room.

'Anyway, he can't spell. I'm much better than him. You should have seen him, Grandad, with his stupid Snap dance. It looked more like he had ants in his pants.'

Billy jumped up and jiggled about, making exaggerated movements. Jacko joined in by woofing.

'Billy, this isn't like you. Come on; sit down.' Grandad tapped the seat beside him. 'You had fun doing the advert, even though you didn't win. You'll have to think of another way to show what you can do. And there's no need to take your frustration out on the TV remote!'

'Come on, Jacko; we need to go. Mum will have gotten home by now.' Billy grabbed the dog's collar and marched him into the kitchen. 'Bye, Grandad,' he said, not sounding sincere.

'Just a minute,' Grandad called after him, but too late — the back door clunked shut.

Billy waited by the garden gate. He looked down the road toward Ant's house; Grandad lived two doors down. With Ant not in sight, he set off up the road toward home.

'Right, Jacko, quick—in case Ant sees us.' Billy pulled on the lead, and Jacko picked up the pace. When he rounded the corner, Billy spotted two boys in the distance, cycling toward him.

'Look, I bet that's Ant. I hope he gets a puncture.' Billy yanked on the lead and dashed across the road without looking.

The sound of a blaring horn stopped him in his tracks. The number 42 bus had just moved off from the stop outside Ant's house.

From the cab, the driver shouted but managed to avoid both boy and dog. 'Look where you're going, or you'll get yourself killed!'

After ducking into the alley opposite, Billy watched the two boys ride past before they disappeared into Ant's garden. 'And good riddance,' he muttered to himself. Billy continued toward his house, thinking all the way about how he could get back at Ant.

Billy banged shut the back door.

'Well, how did it go?' Billy's mum stood busy cooking. 'You're just in time.' She held up a potato peeler. 'You can do these while you tell me about your day.'

Billy dropped his school bag and jacket on the kitchen floor.

'Do I have to?' He mooched over to the sink, where his mum had set a bowl of water, a saucepan, some potatoes, and a peeler.

'Not before you pick up your things.' She pointed at his bag and coat.

'Okay.' Billy snatched up the items and disappeared from the kitchen.

Billy's mum waited for him to return, but he didn't. Instead, she heard his bedroom door slam. 'What's happened, Jacko?'

On hearing his name, the dog wagged his tail. He looked up at her, then at his bowl.

'Here you go.' She emptied a can of dog food into it.

'Billy!' his mum called. 'Come down here.' Billy's mum listened for his footsteps, but none came. She walked to the bottom of the stairs. 'Billy!' she shouted more forcefully.

He appeared on the landing. 'What?'

'Don't *what* me. Come down here, now.'

The look on her face told him she wouldn't back down.

While Billy explained to his mum what had happened, his chest tightened, and his jaw clenched. He felt more determined than ever to get back at Ant.

'We didn't actually do the show,' Billy went on. 'Basically, it was all Ant's fault. He ate all the Krispies, drank the milk, and left his Snap hat at home. He messed up big style, Mum.' That ought to convince her.

Billy checked out his mum's face; she seemed to believe him. 'But Miss gave him a prize anyway for being the most helpful team member.' He dropped a peeled potato into the saucepan, splashing water everywhere.

'My dog was the bestest ever, weren't you Jacko?' He smiled down at the retriever.

'That's odd,' his mum said. 'Sally, I mean Miss Tompkins, is usually very fair. Are you sure nothing else happened?'

'I don't know. Maybe Miss felt sorry for him.' Billy continued with his made-up story. 'He came into school looking like he'd been crying. He said his mum had shouted at him for not being able to tie his shoelaces. And Max told me she'd had to rescue him from a large flying buzzy thing in his bedroom.'

'That doesn't sound right. He'll be ten

soon.' Billy's mum placed the saucepan of potatoes on the hob.

'Max also told me that she watched the Krispies advert and wrote the words for us to learn 'cos Ant can't spell.'

'Does Miss know any of this? Poor Ant.'

'It's not poor Ant. He got the prize, and it should have been me,' Billy insisted as he dried his hands on his trousers.

7

RUMOURS AND LIES

As usual for a Saturday, many of the town's youth met at the shopping centre. Billy locked his bike in the cycle rack and sauntered toward the big mechanical clock. At nearly midday, everyone had gathered beneath it to watch the wooden soldiers march when it struck twelve.

'Hi, Billy,' Tom called to him. 'Why aren't you with Ant?'

'Haven't seen Turner since yesterday. I don't know why you hang around with him.' Billy walked on toward Boards and

Bikes, the skateboard shop. He hoped that Dan or Woody, his other mates, would be there.

Tom caught up with him. 'What's wrong with Ant?'

'Now he's won that prize, he'll be a right pain. You wait, it will be all, I did this, Miss said that, look at me. And do you know what?' Billy turned to Tom, 'He did none of it!'

'Course he did; you were there.' Tom furrowed his brow so hard that his eyebrows looked like he had a woolly caterpillar stuck to his forehead.

Billy exaggerated, 'Yeah, but the real stuff like writing down the words of the advert off the telly and working out the props and things, Max did. She should have won the prize. The only thing Turner did was make Jacko jump off the table and ruin the whole thing.'

Confused, Tom left Billy and headed back to the seats under the big clock. Several of his classmates had grouped there, including Khalid and Julie.

'You okay, Tom?' Khalid spoke in the squeaky toddler voice that he'd used in the Haribo advert. 'Pity about yesterday. Shame Jacko did a runner; otherwise, you might have won.' He laughed along with the rest.

'Yeah, such a shame,' Julie joined in, using her silly voice. 'Well, at least Ant won a prize. So, you sort of did okay.'

'Yeah, but he shouldn't have,' Khalid

remarked, looking around at the group. 'Apparently, he didn't do any of the work; it was all his sister.'

'That's what I heard. She did everything, actually,' Julie said.

'Who told you that?' Tom felt even more confused.

'Your sister; she's friends with Max. They're in the same class.' Julie went on.

'Did Max actually say that she did all the work?' Tom sounded unconvinced.

Julie nodded. 'But I'm not that sure. Katie did say something about Billy telling her ...'

'Quick, shush; here he comes.' Khalid bobbed his head toward the glass doors of the shopping centre.

Ant came through and ambled over

when he saw his classmates.

'Hi, Ant,' Julie squeaked in her silly voice. They all laughed. 'You here to spend your book token?'

He reached into his pocket and pulled it out for everyone to see. 'Do you know if Miss wants us to buy a particular book?'

Julie looked at Khalid, who shrugged. 'I don't think so. I haven't.' She held up a glossy book covered in pictures of her favourite boy band.

'Shouldn't you be getting a book for Max? She did all the work, I hear.' Khalid looked directly at Ant.

'What? What do you mean?' Ant turned to Tom for support. 'I did the lot. It was my idea. I sorted out the stuff, made the dinosaur spines for Jacko, and everything.

Who said I didn't?' He looked at each of them in turn. 'Come on, Tom; you know I did it all.'

'Billy told me.' Tom looked at the ground. 'He says it's your fault that we didn't win, and that you made Jacko jump off the stage.'

Ant slumped down in his seat and dropped his head forward, trying to make sense of what he had heard, and to understand why his best mate would say that.

'Katie knows as well, and she's friends with Max, so it must be true,' Julie said.

'It's not. None of it is.' Ant jumped up and ran for the shopping centre exit.

Billy wandered back toward the clock.

Khalid, Tom, Julie, and several others from his year all stood huddled together. The conversation looked lively, but he couldn't hear what they said.

Tom spotted him coming. 'Billy,' he called out to him. 'You just missed Ant. He ran off when we asked him about Max.'

'See, I told you.' Billy ambled on, heading for the cycle rack.

Max and her mum sat at the kitchen table. Max read aloud from her favourite book, Charlie and the Chocolate Factory.

'Mr Willy Wonka is the most amazing, the most fantastic, the most ...' Max pointed to the page, 'Mum, what's this word, ectordany?'

'Extraordinary.'

'… extraordinary chocolate maker the world has ever seen!'

The crashing sound of the back door bursting open stopped her. Ant appeared. He had tear-stained cheeks, his eyes looked red and puffy, and his nose needed blowing.

'Ant!' His mum jumped up, 'What's happened?' She took a tissue from her pocket and sat him at the table. 'Why are you crying? Hey, you can tell your mum.' After bending at the waist, she brought her face close to his.

'It's …' He sniffed loudly.

'Here.' His mum passed him a tissue, 'Give your nose a good blow.'

'Billy.'

'What about Billy?'

'He's …' Ant's chin wobbled.

'Just breathe slowly and deeply. It'll help you calm down.' His mum stroked the back of his head.

'He's told everyone that Max did the stuff for our advert, and that I shouldn't have won the prize.' He blew his nose again. 'It's not fair.'

Ant looked up at his mum. 'She helped get the words off the telly, but I did everything else.'

'He's said this to everyone, you say?' His mum looked at Max to see if she could confirm his story.

Max shrugged.

'Yeah, down at the shopping centre. They all know. Now, they think I'm a cheat, and I'm not, Mum, really.' Ant sniffed again.

She put her arm around his shoulder. 'Do you think he's jealous of your prize?'

Ant shook his head. 'Dunno.'

'Well, tell me everything that's happened, and I'll phone his mum. She'll know what's going on.'

8

WE ARE ALL DIFFERENT

Billy's mum pressed the 'end call' button on the telephone. She stopped to think about the conversation that she'd just had with Ant's mum.

'Billy,' she called out, standing at the bottom of the stairs. 'Can you come down here, please?'

By the time she had walked back to the kitchen, Jacko had made it down the stairs. She looked at the dog. 'Where is he, Jacko?'

'What?' Billy demanded as he stomped

into the kitchen.

'Sit.' His mum pointed to a chair. Jacko obeyed her, thinking that she'd directed the command at him. 'And you, Billy.'

Then Billy's mum stood and gave him a hard look. 'Now, I've just had a difficult phone call with Ant's mum. She's upset, and so is Ant. Apparently, you've gone around telling stories and starting rumours about him. ... No, don't drop your head; look at me. What have you got to say?' His mum sat herself down on the opposite side of the table.

'Nothing.' Billy looked at Jacko.

'I'm over here. Now, let's try again. Have you told lies about Ant?' Billy's mum held him in her gaze.

'Maybe.' Billy's mumble sounded

unclear.

'Why, for goodness sake? He's your friend.'

'Yeah, well, he won the book token. It's not fair.'

'So, how will lying help?' His mum asked.

''Cos Miss might take it back. It should have been my prize.'

'What makes you say that?'

'I'm better than him.'

'I'm not so sure. For now, I want you to think about what you've said, and then we'll talk some more. In the meantime, set the table. And don't forget, Grandad's coming for tea.'

The click of cutlery on crockery made for the only sound at the table. The grownups sat exchanging glances while Billy pushed his lasagne around his plate. He hadn't spoken a word since the earlier conversation with his mum.

'Come on, Billy lad; what's the matter? You've a face longer than a horse's. Cheer up. It can't be that bad.' Grandad looked at Billy's mum and dad in turn. They both nodded. 'I'll tell you what, Billy; finish off your tea, and we'll go and have a chat, just you and me. How does that sound?'

Billy didn't shift his gaze from his plate.

'Billy, go on; answer your grandad.' His dad sounded stern.

'Yes.' His answer came out as little more than a whisper.

'He can't hear that,' his mum reminded him. 'Speak louder.'

'Yes.'

'Right, so if you're ready.' Grandad pushed back his chair.

Both Billy and his grandad disappeared into the front room.

'Now, sit yourself down here beside me.' Grandad patted the sofa. 'I've had a long chat with your mum, and she's told me everything.' He stopped talking to check on Billy. 'Now, there's no need to worry; we just need to sort this out.

'I knew on Friday that you felt unhappy with Ant after he won and you didn't, but spreading rumours and lies is not at all nice. I know you don't need me to remind you of that.'

Billy nodded.

'What you need to learn from this is that everyone is different: not just in the obvious ways like boy or girl, older or younger, black or white, but also on the inside, too. By that, I mean the way we think, how we see things, and what we are good or not so good at. You, for example, are better at maths, science, and skateboarding, while other children can use their hands to draw, play the piano, or make things.' Grandad looked at Billy to see how he reacted to what he'd said.

'Without differences—' He went on. '— the world would be nothing like it is today. Differences lead to inventions, new ways of doing things, scientific discoveries, and much, much more. What's happening with you and Ant is that you're finding out what you can do well and realising it's different from him.'

Billy's granddad rubbed his chin with his knuckles. 'As I said, you like maths and skateboarding, and Ant's not good at spelling. But, obviously, he's great at organising, thinking up ideas, and being creative, as this advert project has shown. Do you understand what I'm saying?'

He waited for Billy to respond before continuing.

'Suppose so.'

'Well, you need to. As you two get older, you will notice even more differences. And behaving in a nasty way is not the answer. You need to accept and encourage your friends, not get jealous of them. That way, you can concentrate on the things you like doing and excel at.' Grandad lifted Billy's head so that he could look directly into his eyes. 'Does that make sense?'

Billy thought long and hard about what Grandad had said. He realised he'd been mean to Ant, and that he should have felt happy for his friend instead of wanting to take all the attention for himself.

'Can I go now?' Billy shuffled his bottom forward on the sofa. 'I've got something I need to do.'

Billy pulled up outside Ant's house and used the front light of his bike like a torch. He shone it at Ant's bedroom window, waving it around to attract his friend's attention.

A face appeared at the glass, and then disappeared just as quickly. A few seconds later, Ant called from the side of the house. He had run down the stairs and out of the back door.

'Is that you, Tom?' Ant asked as he walked toward the light.

'No, it's me.' Billy didn't sound like his usual self. His voice sounded quiet and controlled as if talking to a grown-up rather than a mate.

The blade of torchlight swung toward Ant's face.

'What do you want?' Ant straightened his spine and pulled his shoulders back. When he spoke again, he sounded annoyed, 'I didn't expect to see you around here.'

'I got to thinking. I want to say sorry for what I said. You weren't to blame for us losing, and Miss was right to give you the prize.'

Ant pushed at the light. 'Get it out of my face.'

Billy switched off the torch. In the orange glow of the street lamp, the friends could see one another clearly.

Ant crossed his arms. 'Why should I believe you? You've been horrible, saying nasty things, telling lies, and for nothing.'

'I know now, and that's why I've come. I had a long chat with my grandad, and he explained about people being different and how that's a good thing.'

'What does he mean, different?'

'Like us. I'm good at maths and science, whereas you're good at thinking things up and organising. It doesn't mean that we can't get better at stuff we find difficult, but you deserved the prize, and I should have felt happy for you. I got jealous and angry because I thought it should have been me. Sorry, mate.'

Billy put his hand on Ant's shoulder. 'Let's go back to being friends like before.'

'No, not like before,' Ant said.

'But ...' Billy drew a breath. 'I've said sorry.'

'Yeah, but as friends *with* our differences.' Ant smiled.

'That reminds me,' Billy said. 'Did you hear about the man whose whole left side got cut off? He's all right now.'

'Yeah, as you say, Billy, let's stick to what we're good at. Joke telling isn't for you!'

THE END

GET YOUR FREE ACTIVITY BOOK

To accompany all of the Billy Books there is a free activity book for each title. Each book includes word search, crossword, secret message, maze and cryptogram puzzles plus pictures to colour.

To get your **free** Activity Book go to **www.thebillybooks.co.uk** and click the button **Get Your Free Activity Book**. Then click the cover of the book matching this book

BOOK REVIEW

If you found this book helpful, leaving a review on Goodreads.com or other book related websites would be much appreciated by me and others who have yet to find it.

WHAT CHILDREN CAN LEARN FROM 'BILLY IS NASTY TO ANT'

In this book, we discuss jealousy. Jealousy, envy, and resentment feel very similar. They are all based on wanting something for ourselves that someone else has, or feeling that we have lost something or are missing something that we deserve. We see things only from our point of view.

As children, one way we learn about ourselves is by making comparisons with what other people have. It could be something physical, such as a new bike or the latest toy, or something emotional, like attention or love.

Jealousy, typically, involves another person. We believe in some way that the thing we want and do not have rightly belongs to us and not to someone else. We may not understand totally whether we actually want it for ourselves, or simply that we don't want the other person to have it. In either case, all we know is that it's not fair that they have it and we don't.

Resentment can follow when we question why we don't have this thing and why the other person has, which can lead to feelings of anger. What we then want is to harm and bring unhappiness to the other person at whatever cost. Although we think we are in the right, these emotions can also lead to feelings of guilt and shame, as we know deep down that we are actually harming the other person by our actions. Unfortunately, jealousy only harms the person who feels it, and if it is not dealt with, it can sometimes last a lifetime.

In the story, Billy thinks he deserves the most attention and a prize because he sees himself as the better student. When Ant receives both, he feels jealous. It doesn't seem fair, and he's afraid he will lose his popularity when Ant becomes the centre of attention. As things progress, he blames Ant for how he feels and wants to get his own back. He tries to turn people against his friend, even telling lies, but of course, Ant hasn't done anything wrong!

Billy only thinks about himself and doesn't consider his friend at all. This continues until Grandad's wisdom helps him understand that we should accept that there are times when others may be more deserving than us. We're all different, and some people prove better at certain things than others.

If you put yourself in the position of the other person, it can help you think about your actions and behaviours. How would you feel if you had achieved something you were proud of, and your friend became angry and resentful instead of being happy for you? That's how Ant felt.

We should all want the best for our friends and family and encourage them when they achieve. Their achievement is not a reflection on us, rather an opportunity to strive for more for ourselves. Then we can expect the same when we do well.

The jealous are troublesome to others, but a torment to themselves. **William Penn**

The worst part of success is trying to find someone who is happy for you. **Bette Midler**

READ ON FOR A TASTER OF

BOOK 4

BILLY AND ANT LIE

James Minter

Helen Rushworth – Illustrator

www.thebillybooks.co.uk

1

THE JOURNEY TO SCHOOL

The downhill ride to Ant's house, though not far, gave enough distance for a keen cyclist to get up a good speed with little effort. Billy always enjoyed this part of his morning journey to school. To feel the wind on his face, the rush of air pulling at his helmet, and the flapping of his bright yellow road safety jacket all added to his sense of excitement. When he travelled so free and fast, he felt like a bird gliding over the ground. The feeling passed, though, when the bus stop opposite Ant's house came into view.

Billy reached for his back brake lever. His fingers hovered over the shiny metal, waiting for the right time to squeeze. Experience had taught him that if he left it until the last moment and applied his brake really hard, he could get the back wheel to lock tight, sending the bike into a skid on the gravelly surface. Billy had practised many times and, most days, could manage at least a two-metre slide.

The gravel littering the bus stop came from passing cars, as their spinning wheels threw up small chippings. It made the surface extra slippery, and the noise of the stones gave a satisfying crunch while he skidded. Billy came to a sudden halt, and a dust cloud rose up behind him. The skid left a black rubber tyre mark on the road.

Billy looked across to Ant's house and, in particular, at his bedroom window. He hoped Ant had stood looking out for him to see today's slide. It turned out he had. Ant responded with a thumbs-up to show his approval before disappearing from view. Within a couple of minutes, Ant reappeared from the side of his house complete with bike, school bag, jacket, and safety gear. He walked across the road to the spot where Billy sat proudly on his bike.

'That was awesome. Look at the tyre mark.' Ant pointed it out on the ground, although he had no need. It looked like a perfect example and clear for anyone to see. 'Here,' Ant said, pushing his handlebars toward Billy. 'Hold this, mate.'

Billy took hold of Ant's bike, thinking he needed both hands free to finish getting ready. Instead, Ant squatted down and pushed at the gravel next to the slide mark. As he brushed away the stones, Billy realised what Ant had found.

Ant held up a pound coin. 'I guess someone must have dropped it when they looked for their bus fare. What a bit of luck.' He slid it into his pocket.

'Oi, that's partly mine. My skid uncovered it.'

'Yeah, but I found it.' Ant shook his head in protest.

'But we're mates. Fifty-fifty, I reckon.'

Billy patted Ant on the shoulder.

Ant snapped shut the safety clip on his cycle helmet. 'I know; let's go to the shop at the garage and get some sweets. We can share them easier than a pound coin.'

'Do we have time before school?' Billy looked at his watch. 'It's eight-forty.'

'If we keep it quick.' Ant checked up and down the road to make sure it was clear. 'Come on, slowcoach.'

Billy soon caught up to him. 'So, what do you fancy? Starburst or Haribos?'

'I dunno. Let's see what we can get for a quid.' Ant peddled on.

They reached the main road. The garage stood on the far side, and the rush hour traffic moved bumper to bumper. The only safe way over was via the pelican crossing.

As they reached it, the red man showed.

Billy got to the button first and pressed it.

'Come on,' Ant said to the lights, pressing the button several more times. 'Hurry up, or we'll be late.'

'It won't help.' Billy hadn't finished speaking before the man turned green, accompanied by the familiar beeping sound of the safe-to-cross signal.

The garage forecourt had three rows of petrol pumps, an area for lorries to fill up with diesel, an automated car wash, a place to pump up tyres or vacuum a car's interior, and an assortment of display shelving complete with newspapers, bunches of flowers, piles of logs for firewood, and stacks of barbeque coals. It had people and vehicles everywhere.

The boys wove in and out of the cars and their owners and pushed their bikes toward the pile of logs. They left them padlocked together and set off to buy some sweets.

The door to the shop, a large single pane of glass, opened inward. Though it stood closed, through it, Billy and Ant could see the long queue waiting to get served.

'Look, it's eight-forty-five.' Billy held out his watch arm. 'We'll end up late.'

'Yeah, but we're here now. Anyway, Miss won't notice. We can sneak in at the back of the assembly hall.' Ant leant in to push on the door.

From inside the shop, Ant heard a shout

of, 'Stop, thief!'

As Ant's hand touched the glass of the door, it exploded into a thousand pieces. The cascade of glass didn't fall downward but blasted outward, pushed from the other side by a person desperate to escape the shop in a hurry.

'Get out of my way!' the person shrieked.

Ant got knocked aside and tumbled backward into the shelf of vases that held several bunches of flowers. Unable to support his weight, the vases with flowers fell to the ground along with him.

Instinctively, Billy covered his face to protect it from the flying fragments. The running man had sent him flying toward the petrol pumps. A car sat at the pump, filling up, and Billy bounced off the front wing, back toward the shop.

He tripped over Ant, and both boys lay in a tangled heap of arms, legs, school bags, and broken vases, each covered in a variety of coloured flowers.

Mayhem broke out inside the shop. An assistant burst through the broken door, shouting "stop him" while waving and pointing at the disappearing figure. Behind the counter, other assistants stood glued to the many CCTV monitors as the robber fled across the forecourt and toward the rush-hour traffic. They scribbled notes, determined to get as much information about the man as they could—hair colour, what he wore, and his height and build—

anything to help the police find him.

Other staff dealt with the impatient customers focused on getting to work. Like a rugby scrum, they pushed forward, insisting on getting served next. The whole scene took place to the shrill, piercing sounds of the alarm triggered by the breaking glass. Shouts from Mr. Gupta, the petrol station manager, added to the racket while he tried to reassure everyone that they had the situation under control.

'You okay?' Billy pulled himself into a crouching position. 'Man, that felt scary.' He brushed at his clothes. Pieces of glass, broken stems, petals, and leaves fell to the ground. 'We'd better get out of here.'

Ant offered him his arm. 'Give us a

hand.'

'You all right, boys?' a chap asked as he came across from the direction of the pumps. 'You were lucky not to have gotten hurt.' He bent and lifted Billy then Ant into a standing position.

'Thanks.' Billy shot Ant a look. 'Yeah, we're fine. Just need to get to school.' Billy looked guarded. 'He's Mr Glenn, the school gardener!' he whispered from behind his hand.

'Can you hear that?' The man turned toward the main road. 'Look at all those flashing lights and sirens. I reckon the whole town's emergency services have turned out.'

Billy and Ant nodded to each other and ran. 'We sooo need to get out of here.'

When Mr Glenn turned back, there remained no sign of the boys. How odd. Oh well, they must be all right.

I HOPE YOU ENJOYED THIS FREE CHAPTER. TO FIND OUT WHAT HAPPENS NEXT CONTINUE READING BOOK 4 'BILLY AND ANT LIE' ...

FOR PARENTS, TEACHERS, AND GUARDIANS; ABOUT THE 'BILLY BOOKS' SERIES

Billy and his friends are children entering young adulthood, trying to make sense of the world around them. Like all children, they are confronted by a complex, diverse, fast-changing, exciting world full of opportunities, contradictions, and dangers through which they must navigate on their way to becoming responsible adults.

What underlies their journey are the values they gain through their experiences. In early childhood, children acquire their values by watching the behaviour of their parents. From around eight years old onwards, children are driven by exploration, and seeking independence; they are more outward looking. It is at this age they begin to think for themselves, and are capable of putting their own meaning to feelings, and the events and experiences they live through. They are developing their own identity.

The Billy Books series supports an initiative championing Values-based Education, (VbE) founded by Dr Neil Hawkes*. The VbE objective is to influence a child's capacity to succeed in life by encouraging them to adopt positive values that will serve them during their early lives, and sustain them throughout their adulthood. Building on the VbE objective, each Billy book uses the power of traditional storytelling to contrast negative behaviours with positive outcomes to illustrate, guide, and shape a child's understanding of the importance of values.

This series of books help parents, guardians and teachers to deal with the issues that challenge children who are coming of age. Dealt with in a gentle way through storytelling, children begin to understand the challenges they face, and the importance of introducing positive values into their everyday lives. Setting the issues in a meaningful context helps a child to see things from a different perspective. These books act as icebreakers, allowing easier communication between parents, or other significant adults, and children when it comes to discussing difficult subjects. They are suitable for KS2, PSHE classes.

There are eight books are in the series. Suggestions for other topics to be dealt with in this way are always welcome. To this end, contact the author by email: james@jamesminter.com.

*Values-Based Education, (VbE) is a programme that is being adopted in schools to inspire adults and pupils to embrace and live positive human values. In English schools, there is now a Government requirement to teach British values. More information can be found at: www.valuesbasededucation.com/

BOOK 1 - BILLY HAS A BIRTHDAY

Bullies appear confident and strong. That is why they are scary and intimidating. Billy loses his birthday present, a twenty-pound note, to the school bully. With the help of a grown-up, he manages to get it back and the bully gets what he deserves.

BOOK 2 - BILLY AND ANT FALL OUT

False pride can make you feel so important that you would rather do something wrong than admit you have made a mistake. In this story, Billy says something nasty to Ant and they row. Ant goes away and makes a new friend, leaving Billy feeling angry and abandoned. His pride will not let him apologise to his best friend until things get out of hand.

BOOK 3 - BILLY IS NASTY TO ANT

Jealousy only really hurts the person who feels it. It is useful to help children accept other people's successes without them feeling vulnerable. When Ant wins a school prize, Billy can't stop himself saying horrible things. Rather than being pleased for Ant, he is envious and wishes he had won instead.

BOOK 4 - BILLY AND ANT LIE

Lying is very common. It's wrong, but it's common. Lies are told for a number of different reasons, but one of the most frequent is to avoid trouble. While cycling to school, Billy and Ant mess around and lie about getting a flat tyre to cover up their lateness. The arrival of the police at school regarding a serious crime committed earlier that day means their lie puts them in a very difficult position.

BOOK 5 - BILLY HELPS MAX

Stealing is taking something without permission or payment. Children may steal for a dare, or because they want something and have no money, or as a way of getting attention. Stealing shows a lack of self-control. Max sees some go-faster stripes for her bike. She has to have them, but her birthday is ages away. She eventually gives in to temptation.

BOOK 6 - BILLY SAVES THE DAY

Children need belief in themselves and their abilities, but having an inflated ego can be detrimental. Lack of self-belief holds them back, but overpraising leads to unrealistic expectations. Billy fails to audition for the lead role in the school play, as he is convinced he is not good enough.

BOOK 7- BILLY WANTS IT ALL

The value of money is one of the most important subjects for children to learn and carry with them into adulthood, yet it is one of the least-taught subjects. Billy and Ant want skateboards, but soon realise a reasonable one will cost a significant amount of money. How will they get the amount they need?

BOOK 8 - BILLY KNOWS A SECRET

You keep secrets for a reason. It is usually to protect yourself or someone else. This story explores the issues of secret-keeping by Billy and Ant, and the consequences that arise. For children, the importance of finding a responsible adult with whom they can confide and share their concerns is a significant life lesson.

MULTIPLE FORMATS

Each of the Billy books is available as a **paperback**, as a **hardback** including coloured pictures, as **eBooks** and in **audio**-book format.

COLOURING BOOK

The Billy Colouring book is perfect for any budding artist to express themselves with fun and inspiring designs. Based on the Billy Series, it is filled with fan-favourite characters and has something for every Billy, Ant, Max and Jacko fan.

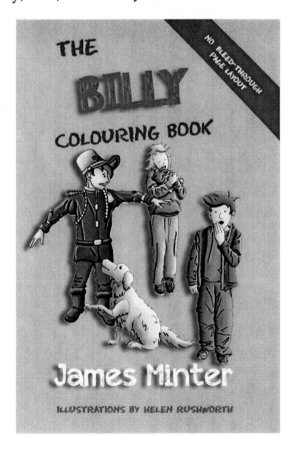

THE BILLY BOOKS COLLECTIONS
VOLUME 1 AND 2

For those readers who cannot wait for the next book in the series, books 1, 2, 3, and 4 are combined into a single work — The Billy Collection, Volume 1, whilst books 5, 6, 7, and 8 make up Volume 2.

The collections are still eligible for the free activity books. Find them all at www.thebillybooks.co.uk .

ABOUT THE AUTHOR

I am a dad of two grown children and a stepfather to three more. I started writing five years ago with books designed to appeal to the inner child in adults - very English humour. My daughter Louise, reminded me of the bedtime stories I told her and suggested I write them down for others to enjoy. I haven't yet, but instead, I wrote this eight-book series for 7 to 9-year-old boys and girls. They are traditional stories dealing with negative behaviours with positive outcomes.

Although the main characters, Billy and his friends, are made up, Billy's dog, Jacko, is based on our much-loved family pet, which, with our second dog Malibu, caused havoc and mayhem to the delight of my children and consternation of me.

Prior to writing, I was a college lecturer and later worked in the computer industry, at a time before smartphones and tablets, when computers were powered by steam and stood as high as a bus.

WEBSITES

www.thebillybooks.co.uk

www.jamesminter.com

E-MAIL

james@jamesminter.com

TWITTER

@james_minter

FACEBOOK

facebook.com/thebillybooks/

facebook.com/author.james.minter

ACKNOWLEDGEMENTS

Like all projects of this type, there are always a number of indispensable people who help bring it to completion. They include Christina Lepre, for her editing and incisive comments, suggestions and corrections. Harmony Kent for her proofreading, and Helen Rushworth of Ibex Illustrations, for her images that so capture the mood of the story. Gwen Gades for her cover design. And Maggie, my wife, for putting up with my endless pestering to read, comment and discuss my story, and, through her work as a personal development coach, her editorial input into the learnings designed to help children become responsible adults.